REA

MR.
THUNDERMUG

'I could never look long upon a monkey, without very mortifying reflections.'

William Congreve

MR.
THUNDERMUG

CORNELIUS MEDVEI

HarperCollins*Publishers*

HarperCollins books may be purchased for educational, business, or sales
promotional use. For information please write: Special Markets Department,
HarperCollins Publishers, 10 East 53rd Street, New York, NY 10022.

Published in Great Britain in 2006 by Fourth Estate.

FIRST U.S. EDITION

Illustrations by the author.

Library of Congress Cataloging-in-Publication Data is available upon
request.

ISBN: 978-0-06-114612-1
ISBN-10: 0-06-114612-9

07 08 09 10 11 ❖ / RRD 10 9 8 7 6 5 4 3 2 1

1

ONE RAINY NIGHT not long ago, a curious report appeared in the late edition of our city's evening newspaper. Under the headline 'MONKEY PROFESSOR DIES', it was the obituary notice for an academic, one Dr Alphonsus Rotz. The article went like this:

DR ALPHONSUS ROTZ, who has died at the age of 60, was one of the most original zoologists of recent years. He will be best remembered for his fieldwork with primates.

After taking a degree in zoology, followed by a Ph.D. on 'Posterior Pigmentation in the Mandrill', Alphonsus Rotz was appointed Extraordinary Research Fellow at the National University, allowing him a generous stipend that provided the basis for a series of audacious research projects.

Probably the most famous of these projects was his 19-year period of unorthodox and, at times, controversial field research on the silver-maned baboons of the Ethiopian savannah. He went there with a party of graduate students, which he was supervising on a summer project. At the end of the summer his students returned home, but Rotz decided to stay. Left alone, he extended the theory of total immersion fieldwork, already practised widely by forward-thinking anthropologists. He became part of the baboon colony, living in a cave in the rocks, sharing their diet of roots and insects and taking part in their courtship rituals. Years later, Dr Rotz recalled in an interview how he had gained the creatures' trust so completely that baboon mothers would give him their offspring to suckle when they went out hunting.

But Dr Rotz's uncompromising approach to fieldwork had its drawbacks. Cut off as he was, the project leaders heard from him less and less frequently, and eventually Rotz lost all contact with the academic establishment. Assuming he was dead, the university stopped paying his stipend.

However, Dr Rotz was not dead, and he had even

been contributing sporadically to a journal published in Addis Ababa. The back numbers of this publication give an idea of the work he was engaged in among the baboons. At first he was interested in routine questions, such as the animals' diet and etiquette, and the significance of the baboon in local folklore. Later articles contained outlines for a theory on the origin of language, and a detailed study of baboon vocal cords.

After nineteen years Dr Rotz left the savannah abruptly and returned home, to the astonishment and delight of his colleagues. He was unkempt and incoherent, and he brought with him only a small package containing his journals and a few mementos – a lock of pungent-smelling hair and a greasy photograph of a baboon baring its teeth. It was never fully explained why he had chosen, after all this time, to break off his research and come home. All Dr Rotz would say was that he had left for 'personal reasons'.

Only at this point in the article did Dr Rotz's – admittedly tenuous – connection with our city become clear. When he returned from Africa, his former colleagues were naturally pleased to see that he was still alive, but having once stopped his stipend the university authorities were reluctant to start paying it again, and so Dr Rotz left to take up the position of visiting professor of zoology at the Central University of our city. The obituary continued:

DURING THIS TIME he published a series of papers which synthesized his findings and his theories from his work among the baboons. One of these papers gained particular notoriety in academic circles. In it he described how he had run a kind of hedge school for baboons with the purpose of identifying the most intelligent animals at an early age. He had worked with one unusually gifted female over a period of several years and eventually succeeded – so he claimed – in teaching the animal to speak. The appendix to this paper contained a lyrical account, quite unsuitable for an academic essay, of their long discussions of German Romantic poetry, sitting on a rocky outcrop in the moonlight, overlooking the boundless savannah.

After some deliberation the university authorities agreed to publish this paper, but in the storm of controversy that followed its appearance, they must have regretted their decision. When Dr Rotz proposed a further article entitled 'Some thoughts on Homo-baboonus', which was to consider the possibility of cross-breeding between humans and baboons, they turned him down without hesitation.

Dr Rotz had his new paper published privately, but after this it was almost impossible for him to find another job in a university. When his visiting professorship came to an end he returned to his home town, where he worked in a primary school. He taught arithmetic, geography and, when no other teachers were looking, Customs of the Great Apes. This made him very popular with the children. His standing rose within the school, and eventually he married the headmistress.

The obvious happiness which this marriage brought him, and his fruitful association with the Primate Society, made the last years of his life a period of quiet productivity. It was during this period that he invented the pongoid exfoliator, a device for removing unwanted skin from the feet of gorillas and chimpanzees.

At the time of his death, Dr Rotz was on an expedition in Brazil, sponsored by the Primate Society.

He was leading a team of researchers investigating one of the largest macaque colonies of the Orinoco when he went missing early last week. The exact circumstances of his death are still unclear, as his body has not been recovered. However, remnants of clothing found in the spot where he disappeared indicate that he was probably eaten by a jaguar.

He is survived by his headmistress; there were no children.

Few people stop to buy the evening paper on a rainy night, and few of them read as far as the obituaries, which appear on the same page as the standing apology for errors and the chess problem, so the number of people in our city who learnt of Dr Alphonsus Rotz's passing was probably very small. I myself know about the obituary only because I was working on the *Evening News* at the time. The editor made a point of showing it to me, because he had the idea that I had once studied at the Central University myself.

As I read the obituary, an absurd picture came to me of Dr Rotz chalking up irregular verbs on a rockface while a troop of baboons clustered attentively round his feet. The obvious conclusion was that Dr Rotz was an eccentric who had been turned by nineteen years of isolation and the rigours of an unfamiliar climate into an out-and-out fantasist. And yet the singlemindedness with which he pursued his academic interests was somehow at odds with this thesis – not to mention his mysterious disappearance among the macaques of the Orinoco, which seemed such a fitting conclusion to a singular life.

I made some enquiries at the Central University, but the few academics who admitted to having known Dr Rotz seemed incapable of agreeing on the most basic details about him. One elderly professor remembered him having a long white beard, while another showed me a photograph of Dr Rotz at a departmental dinner, dark-haired and clean-shaven. There appeared to be no point in investigating the matter further; in any case, I had other assignments to deal with. The obituary was published and forgotten, and I put the whole thing out of my mind.

Later, though, when the first shocking reports about Mr Thundermug began to circulate, I realized I had been fortunate to read that obituary. For the appearance in our city first of Dr Rotz, like a voice crying in the wilderness, and then of Mr Thundermug, the walking vindication of his wildest theories, struck me as being at the very least an extraordinary coincidence. In fact, I was sure at first that the two cases must be linked, like outbreaks of a disease which appear at first to be isolated but are invariably traced to the same source.

I never found any evidence to prove a connection, but I had the idea of presenting the obituary of Dr Rotz, together with all the information I have (mixed with a necessary amount of speculation) about Mr Thundermug, in the hope that one case might shed some light on the other. I don't present this story as a scoop, but rather as a case history, of the kind popular among brain doctors and criminologists. And speaking of criminology, while I was assembling these notes I was given a folder of intriguing photographs by a friend in the Police Department. They appear to have been part of a dossier of evidence – it seems the authorities had been keeping an eye on Mr Thundermug for some time. These photographs are hardly works of art, but when I examined them I noticed that they corroborated various details of my story, and so I have included a selection at relevant points in the text.

2

THIS IS A GREAT CITY, but it was once even greater. Its ancient walls are evidence of this: a massive sinuous rampart, each of its million bricks stamped with the name of its donor. Even today the confusion of shops and shacks and tower blocks and temples and electric cables that is the modern city scarcely spreads beyond the line of the old walls. In some places it has even withdrawn. On the road out of town you might pass through suburban districts of houses, or even through open fields; then suddenly one of the great gates looms up at the end of a street, or you turn in under the shadow of the wall itself – only then do you realize that you have still not crossed the limits of the old city.

The city stands on the bank of a great river, which flows down through the whole country. Its upper reaches

are famous for the beauty of their scenery, for foaming torrents plunging through narrow gorges, but here the river is too wide to be lovely. A bend in its course brings it in directly under the city walls. The narrow strip of land between the walls and the bank is crowded with warehouses, wharves and jetties.

On the other side of the city a mountain rises sharply from the foot of the walls. It is covered with beech and chestnut woods, and considered to be at its most beautiful in autumn, when the red and yellow leaves on its slopes are visible, like a conflagration, from every quarter of the city.

Despite its fortifications, the city has been fired, flooded, sacked and looted many times in its history, and the great walls enclose a perplexing jumble of buildings: cracked flyovers carrying traffic above ancient shrines, air-raid shelters converted into shopping centres, glassy skyscrapers growing out of the rubble of entire districts of flattened houses, unhampered by planning regulations. Within the walls, virtually the only piece of the old fabric that remains intact is the crisscross network of its streets, the straight avenues that run for miles between the gates. These avenues are lined with spreading plane trees whose branches meet across the road. In summer, when the trees are in leaf, it is quite dark underneath, so that in a car you have the curious sensation of driving under water.

The sections between the main streets are crammed with houses and shacks in various stages of disintegration, and riddled with narrow lanes that wind in every direction. To venture down one of these lanes is to join an unending stream of traffic, taxis and bicycles and pedestrians, negotiating your way past a succession of obstacles: past makeshift food stalls, card players at tables on the pavement, old women dozing in chairs, and through the milling crowds of spectators that gather round them. It is easy to get lost here: the lanes and junctions are like so many miles of tangled knitting, and all jammed with the same obstructions, swarming with the same crowds and decorated with the same embellishments of plant-pots and slop-buckets, open manholes, trailing vines and telephone cables.

Down one of these lanes that run crazily between the houses, in front of a heavy wooden door decorated with carvings of flowers, ridged and pitted and shiny with age, a monkey sits on the worn stone step. Beside him is a small pile of melon seeds, which he is cracking one by one between his teeth. The ground at his feet is littered with shells. He has the same air of absorption in his task as the stallholders frying dumplings or the gangs of card players. Leaning back against the door, he glances up occasionally at the stream of passers-by, but they pay no attention to him. An interested person could easily identify him as a baboon from his mane and the shape of his head, although he is unusually big for a baboon.

His heavy, chiselled face is rather like that of the stylized beasts carved in stone that guard so many doorways in this city; perhaps that is why no one pays him any attention. His long dog's muzzle and whiskery cheeks recall those dark portraits of Victorian grandees with their lugubrious expressions and mutton-chop whiskers.

This is his portrait: his head and shoulders are draped in a mane of thick hair that covers his upper body like

a cape, the kind worn by a cyclist in the rain, or by Sherlock Holmes. He has small dark eyes set together under a battering-ram forehead, which gives him an intense, concentrated expression, as if he is grappling with some philosophical problem. Powerful jaws open to reveal a set of surprisingly small teeth, and no lips. On the side of his head turned towards us, half covered by the hair, is an ear shaped like a human's, but far more mobile.

Below the mane his belly and back legs taper away, so that he seems top heavy. His tail is slightly ridiculous: rounded like a piece of rope, with a thick tuft of hair at the end, it sticks up out of the small of his back, revealing his brick-red backside. Between the scrawny legs his thin pink willy hangs down like a hand-grip on an underground train. His paws are perhaps the most remarkable feature of all – almost human hands in miniature, with four delicate fingers and a thumb; but the fat, padded palms with their deep wrinkles and the thick hairs that cover even the backs of the fingers can only be those of an animal.

He cracks another melon seed between his teeth and spits out the shell. Across the lane a little boy, whose mother is buying dumplings at one of the stalls, stares at him. The baboon bares his teeth. 'What are you looking at?' he growls. The little boy continues to stare in fascination. The baboon sighs, cracks another melon seed and begins to scratch his balls.

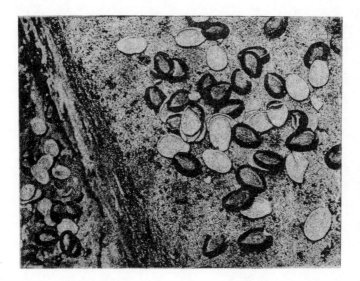

3

NOBODY ever established where it was that the baboon came from, or what had brought him to this unnatural habitat. The basic facts are confusing – clearly, baboons are not native to this region; but, on the other hand, Mr Thundermug spoke our language perfectly, with no trace of an accent, and there is no evidence that he knew any foreign languages.

There were in fact numerous theories as to the baboon's origins, but it was impossible to know which, if any, was true; all they had in common was their lack of supporting evidence. This in itself was not surprising, as our city excels in the manufacture of rumours. Nevertheless, the theories I heard were so often attributed, at various removes, to Mr Thundermug himself, that I began to think the baboon must have taken a perverse delight in providing contradictory accounts of his origins – tailored perhaps to his mood and the company.

There was, for example, the romantic account, in which he and his wife, after a night of love in the open air, had crept away to sleep in a basket which they stumbled on among the dry grasses: it was the basket of a weather balloon that was to be launched the following morning. Their presence went unnoticed at the launch, but once in the air the extra weight of the two baboons drove it off course and instead of going into orbit, as it should have done, the balloon drifted among the clouds until it came to rest somewhere in the vicinity of our city. Then there was the scientific account, according to which the baboon had been created in a laboratory by a renegade professor who stole stuffed animals from museums and brought them to life with a combination of injections and electric shocks.

Perhaps there was a germ of truth in one of these stories, but if so it was well concealed, and so Mr Thundermug's origins remain a mystery. No one ever mentioned the most obvious explanation, that the baboon and his family had simply escaped from a nearby zoo; in any case, it must be ruled out, since most of the zoos in the district had no baboons in their monkey houses, and the two that did never reported any animals missing.

The house occupied by the family was much like the others in the street: it had a roof of black tiles, overhanging eaves, shuttered windows and a balcony. An untidy assortment of potted plants softened the lines of the front step. The woodwork needed painting; the place had been empty until the baboons arrived.

The house was known as Crofty Creek, a name that seemed so odd to me, when I first came across it in a newspaper report, that I was sure it must be a misprint. When I visited the house, though, I saw to the right of the front door a tarnished brass plate bearing the name in capital letters, exactly as spelt in the newspaper. This was odd enough, but I discovered later that the house appears in the records of the City Council only under its number in the street – there is no mention of a name. Perhaps 'Crofty Creek' was a name of Mr Thundermug's own invention.

Of course, there are many empty houses in our city, but I like to think that the baboon chose Crofty Creek out of all the others because of its proximity to a row of banana trees, which grew outside a police station near the east gate of the city. They had been planted on the order of the chief of police, so that on wet days incarcerated criminals could meditate on the sound made by the water battering the huge leaves.

I imagine the baboons' arrival during one of those violent cloudbursts which are so common here during the summer months: they would have picked their way through the suddenly deserted streets, dismayed by the chilly gusts of spray and the water running round their ankles, until they passed under the banana trees, and the raindrops rattled on the leaves with such a dreadful noise that they were moved to look for shelter. They did not go into the police station itself, which was full of policemen, but into the empty house a little way down the street: this was Crofty Creek.

As it happens, the house was not only empty but condemned, due to an infestation of cockroaches which nobody had been able to eradicate. But this would not have deterred the baboons: on the contrary, it was a convenient supply of nourishment. As the rain poured down outside there was a terrible noise of stamping and clattering, and the rustling of alarmed cockroaches. Scrambling up the creaking stairs, over the dusty floorboards, the baboons hunted the little insects all over the house, and soon they had collected enough for a substantial meal. They ate squatting on the kitchen table. Then, tired from their journey, their stomachs laden with cockroaches, they crept upstairs and fell asleep in the bath.

4

MORE puzzling even than the question of his origins was the question of how the baboon had learnt to speak. Of course, if we are to believe the claims of Dr Alphonsus Rotz, Mr Thundermug was not the first baboon in natural history to have learnt human speech. In a way, though, his achievement was even more extraordinary, for while the alleged achievements of Dr Rotz were due to his tireless and brilliant tutoring, Mr Thundermug, as far as anyone knows, had no teacher.

It appears that we are dealing with one of those mysterious upheavals of evolution; a spontaneous kindling of consciousness, in the way a heap of grass clippings will provide the spark to set itself alight. But even this explanation stretches credibility when we consider the size of the leap between the shrieks and grunts of a primate and

the polished and unsettling eloquence of Mr Thundermug
– it seems closer to the impossible tales of men pulling
themselves out of swamps by their own hair.

Surprisingly, perhaps, given their wildly diverse
theories about the baboon's origins, people's accounts of
how he learnt to speak are more or less consistent. This
does little for their credibility – the explanation still strikes
me as profoundly unscientific. In the absence of anything
more convincing, however, I have no alternative but to
reproduce the prevailing theory in full.

SOME time after the baboons' arrival at Crofty Creek,
the smothering heat of late spring closed over the city.
The various street smells, dormant all winter – the smells
of drains and sweat and cheap perfume and rotting
vegetables – sprang to the nostrils with renewed vigour.
The heaps of pineapples at the market stalls were replaced
by melons and small hard peaches. Those citizens who
were able to leave went away, and those who remained
became testy and unpredictable.

Baboons, of course, are naturally designed for the
fierce heat of the savannah. Even so, the male baboon
was finding the interior of Crofty Creek uncomfortable
– perhaps with his thick mane he felt the heat more than

the rest of his family. He had started taking an afternoon nap a little way down the street, under a tree whose dense foliage and spreading branches provided a cool shade even when the sun was directly overhead.

The tree's location, however, was not ideal: it stood in the grounds of a residential home for the irretrievably insane, which meant that the baboon's rest was frequently disturbed. He would curl up between the roots of the tree, or in the crook of a low branch, and doze, listening with one eye open to the conversations of the patients. Usually they talked among themselves, or to themselves, but sometimes he addressed them directly; he bared his teeth if they came too near.

At first the baboon would close his watching eye and go back to sleep when he lost interest in the patients' conversations, but as the days passed he listened with increasing restlessness. The hairs along his spine rose like a dog's, his mane bristled and his bottom dyed itself a violent shade of purple. Eventually he would lose his temper altogether, and shake his backside at the patients, or chase them round the garden with savage barks.

It occurred to me that there might be some value in knowing exactly who spoke to the baboon during these first encounters with humanity – suppose, for example, that one of the patients had provided some vital spur to his acquisition of language? And so I visited the residential home myself to see what I could discover.

The tree under which the baboon had taken his naps was still standing, casting its long shadow across the lawn (it was early in the morning, and the patients were doing their exercises in pyjamas on the grass); but this was the only part of the story I managed to verify. The director appeared to misunderstand my request for information.

'Thought he was a monkey, did he?' she said. 'We don't release details about any of our patients, I'm afraid.'

As for interviewing the patients, to see if they remembered the baboon; the director said that was out of the question. 'You might upset them,' she said.

'What do you mean, "upset them"?'

'You've got exactly the kind of face that would upset them,' she told me.

Whatever the nature of the baboon's encounters with the patients, the life's work of Dr Alphonsus Rotz was about to be substantiated. For it was an irrefutable fact that the baboon had learnt human speech. He no longer simply listened to what the patients said, but answered them and joined in their conversations – although this did not last for long because, it seems, they found his combative manner and caustic wit disturbing. Eventually they began to avoid him altogether.

Ostracized by the patients, the baboon abandoned the residential home and began spending his afternoons in the police station, where he had found a new sleeping place among the spare uniforms on top of a locker in one of the back rooms. Increasingly, however, he was drawn to the more stimulating atmosphere of the officers' common room. This was empty for much of the day, but the television was always on at full volume. The baboon would squat for hours on the window-ledge, absorbing weather reports, dramas, commercials and adding new items to his rapidly expanding vocabulary. One day he came home with names for himself and his family. He called the two children Angus and Trudy after characters in a drama series that he had been watching. For himself he chose the name Mr Thundermug; it was a word he had come across in a documentary programme, although in what context he could not remember.

I find this part of the account unsatisfactory, because it does not explain the elegance of the baboon's speech, which so many people remarked upon – his extensive vocabulary, his mastery of rhetoric. The television may have supplied him with names, but it is hardly credible as the source of such an astonishing facility with language. And, as far as we know, this facility was with him from the beginning, for no one remembers him at an earlier stage of linguistic development communicating, say, in broken phrases mixed with gibbers and howls. It seems the power of speech sprang up in Mr Thundermug complete and fully developed, like the army sown from dragon's teeth.

There is no record of how Mr Thundermug felt about his newly acquired abilities. This is perhaps ironic, given their nature: he was now in a position to provide the first ever account of the inner life of a baboon. But perhaps his animal instincts told him that such an account would draw the immediate and unwelcome attention of zoologists and linguists, pedagogues and philosophers and reporters; so he developed instead a tendency to discretion and obfuscation.

At home in Crofty Creek, it appears that Mr Thundermug wasted valuable hours trying to pass on the secret of human language to his family. But they never managed to understand or utter even the simplest words, and eventually he abandoned his efforts. Of course, they could still communicate in the way they had always done, with shrieks of rage and grunts of enjoyment, mock fights and mutual grooming; and, in the case of Mrs Thundermug, with the old courtship rituals. All the same, these forms of communication must have seemed severely limited to a baboon with all the resources of our language at his disposal, and it is surely reasonable to assume that he felt some degree of frustration and estrangement. If he did, though, Mr Thundermug never mentioned it, and usually made light of the family's failure to learn, putting it down to restricted mental capacities or, when he was in a conciliatory mood, to his own shortcomings as a teacher. What really troubled him, he claimed, was the fact that he was illiterate.

5

A CONSTANT stream of migrants passes through the gates of our city from every corner of the country, to be fed in its canteens, sheltered in its tenements and employed in its factories and on its building sites. A hundred styles of cooking mingle in its kitchens, and the citizens' speech, incorporating as it does influences from all the major dialect regions, is a source of perpetual fascination to philologists. In short, our city is profoundly cosmopolitan in its constitution and its attitudes, so that if there were anywhere an articulate baboon might hope for a favourable reception, it should be here. As it turned out, however, Mr Thundermug's first encounters with his fellow-citizens were frustrating and unsatisfactory.

There was, for example, his visit to the greengrocer's, when he clambered delicately over a pile of melons under

the shop awning, tapping and sniffing until he had iden-
tified a specimen at the very peak of its ripeness; he
called to the assistant to wrap it up for him. It was dark
under the awning, but when the assistant at last made
out the form of Mr Thundermug on top of the melons,
she ran at him without a word and chased him out of
the shop.

The baboon had no more success when he visited the
post office. When his turn came to be served he said
politely, 'Good morning. I would like three first-class
stamps, and this package is to go by registered post to
Whipsnade.' But the postmistress simply ignored him
and turned to the next customer. Flushed with rage, Mr
Thundermug slunk out of the building.

The man at the next counter, who was buying a set
of stamps featuring Endangered Species, stared in amaze-
ment. 'Who was that?' he asked.

'Oh,' said the postmistress, 'that's just an old baboon
that lives round here.'

'But it speaks our language!' the man cried. 'Isn't that
incredible?'

'Doesn't speak it very well,' said the postmistress,
dismissively.

But the man had already rushed outside, forgetting

his commemorative stamps. He caught up with Mr Thundermug a little way down the street. 'Excuse me, sir,' he said, 'I couldn't help hearing what you were saying – wonderful set of vocal cords you have there. My name's Roger Claptrap; I'm a speech therapist – you may have seen my book, *Diphthongs and What They Do*. May I talk to you for a few minutes?'

'No time,' said the baboon, 'terribly busy,' and he began to scamper down the street, so that Mr Claptrap had to run along almost bent double to continue talking to him. But the therapist persisted, and eventually Mr Thundermug allowed himself to be invited to dinner at a nearby restaurant.

'I think I'll have the sole Meunière,' said Mr Claptrap, when the waiter came to take their order. 'What about you?'

'I'll have the same,' said Mr Thundermug, who had been studying the menu with complete incomprehension.

After a while the waiter returned with sole Meunière for Mr Claptrap, and a bunch of bananas, which he placed in front of Mr Thundermug.

'What the hell's this?' began the baboon, dangerously.

'I thought your monkey would probably prefer these bananas,' the waiter said, turning to Mr Claptrap, 'although strictly speaking, sir, you shouldn't have brought it in here, you know.'

'But I ordered the sole Meunière as well,' shouted Mr Thundermug, red-faced with anger.

'Let's swap, shall we?' said the therapist, waving the waiter away and passing his plate to Mr Thundermug. 'As a matter of fact I quite like bananas. I expect he didn't mean any offence.'

'Imbecile,' snorted Mr Thundermug. 'Anyway, bananas don't grow on the savannah.' He ate the sole Meunière with relish, but he was too incensed to give

helpful answers to Mr Claptrap's numerous questions about labials and fricatives, and refused to let him palpate his larynx. Eventually the therapist turned his attention to his food. It must have been some consolation to him that he managed to finish the entire bunch of bananas by himself.

6

IT IS not easy to give a picture of the Thundermugs' early life in Crofty Creek. Their neighbours seem to have been singularly unobservant, and on the one occasion I visited, after the family had left, the door was boarded up and the house already marked for demolition, so I had to be content with peering through the windows and the garden gate. Now, of course, that whole section of the city has been swept away and Mr Thundermug's old neighbourhood is a building site, where the concrete skeletons of thirty-storey towers rise and vanish into the summer drizzle, so there is no chance of investigating any further, and I must do the best I can with the information I have.

The baboons' existence seems to have been divided between foraging for food, eating and sleep: no regular time of day was allotted for these activities, so midnight might equally well find them clattering over the rooftops, ransacking the litter bins near the east gate, squatting over a protracted and heavy meal, or peacefully asleep.

Their material life was simple. The only items of furniture they made use of were the kitchen table, on which they hoarded the surplus from their foraging expeditions, and the bath, in which they slept. The ground-floor rooms (I noticed, peering through the windows) were littered with newspapers, empty bottles, lengths of electric cable, an old mattress propped against a wall; detritus perhaps collected by Mr Thundermug and brought home for further examination.

These are no more than glimpses of a life, but even so it seems that the baboons had succeeded remarkably well in adapting themselves to their new habitat. One of the few details that can be reported with any certainty is the incident which brought this initial period to an end, since it is recorded in the Council archives. One morning Mr Thundermug received a letter; a brown envelope lay on the doormat. He was, of course, unable to read the address, but he assumed, correctly, that it was meant for him. He took it outside, tore it open carefully with his upper left canine and spread it out on the step to look at it.

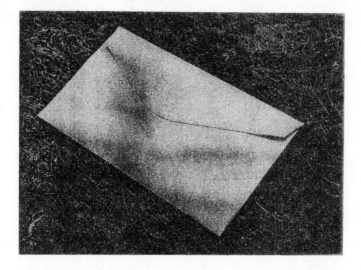

It was a pity that Mr Thundermug could not read, because the letter was important: it came from the Housing Department of the City Council. Although he was occupying one of its properties, the occupier did not appear to be on the Housing Department's list. If he required assistance with finding housing he should register with the Housing Department. Meanwhile, was he aware that he was squatting illegally? The occupier's attention was also drawn to the fact that this property had been declared unfit for human habitation due to an extraordinary infestation of cockroaches. A speedy reply would be appreciated.

Mr Thundermug stared at the letter in frustration for several minutes, then rolled it into a ball and swallowed it.

But the Council was persistent. A few days later there was a knock at the door. Scampering down the hall and squinting discreetly through the letterbox, Mr Thundermug saw a balding man in a sports jacket, and he quickly opened the door, grinning in such a way that all his teeth were visible. The man introduced himself as Mr Forrest, from the City Council Housing Department.

'Did you get our letter?' asked Mr Forrest.

'No letter,' said the baboon. He did not like to admit that the letter had come but that he had been unable to read it.

'You shouldn't be living here,' said Mr Forrest. 'This house is a health hazard. It's full of cockroaches.'

'No, it isn't,' said Mr Thundermug, complacently. 'We ate them all.'

'I find that hard to believe,' said Mr Forrest, with ill-concealed disgust.

'All the same, it's true,' replied the baboon, patting his wizened belly at the memory.

'In that case, we'll have to repossess.'

'I claim squatter's rights,' said Mr Thundermug,

squatting on the doormat and standing up quickly because the bristles stung his backside.

'You can't do that if you broke into the house in the first place.'

'But we didn't break in,' said Mr Thundermug, with great cunning. 'We climbed down the chimney.'

Mr Forrest tried another line of approach. 'What's your date of birth?' he asked.

'I was born under a falling star,' said Mr Thundermug, deciding to be as vague as possible.

'That must have been the Loopy Hop comet,' said Mr Forrest, who was used to this kind of thing, 'which makes you about five years old, and I'll put the exact date down as the first of April. It also means,' he continued triumphantly, 'that you're a minor and we'll have to take you into care.'

'On the contrary,' replied Mr Thundermug, coolly, 'in baboon years I'm three hundred and seventy-eight, so I'm eligible for a pension.'

Mr Forrest went away to place the matter in the hands of a legal expert.

7

Mr Thundermug was not worried by the Council's interest in him. He merely felt a mild satisfaction at having so easily outwitted Mr Forrest, and soon forgot their conversation. A more prudent animal might have considered his legal position or consulted a solicitor; but even if Mr Thundermug had been more prudent, the matter would not have preoccupied him for long, because soon after Mr Forrest's visit the baboon fell ill.

He woke up one morning with a terrible pain in his abdomen. It was hardly surprising, considering the dreadful strain he had undergone in his acquisition of language, that he should have been run down and susceptible to infection. He was probably suffering from some kind of gastric flu – an unpleasant viral infection had recently been emptying the local schools.

He crawled downstairs and lay in the hall, rubbing his belly against the bristles of the doormat, in the hope that this would make the pain go away. When he realized that it was not having any effect, he went shakily outside to look for a phone box. He knew what he had to do, because he had seen several medical dramas on the television in the police station: he must dial the emergency number and ask for an ambulance.

But it happened that the phone boxes in the streets near Crofty Creek were new, and the private company that owned them had not yet got round to installing telephones in them. When he discovered this Mr Thundermug crumpled to the ground in despair, pressing his spine against the cooling metal of the phone box. Sweat trickled down his mane and over his craggy forehead. His face twisted in a snarl of agony, and he fell into a light doze.

He woke a short while later to find a small terrier sniffing busily at his legs, while an old woman in a padded cotton jacket crouched beside him peering into his face and prodding his chest. 'Up you get, old chap,' she said. 'Can you walk?'

'I have a terrible pain in my abdomen,' said Mr Thundermug.

'Well, I think you should see the vet,' said the old woman. And she jumped out into the street and flagged down a passing taxi.

'Thank you, dear lady,' mumbled the baboon, as she opened the door for him. 'Get off me, you carbuncle,' he snapped at the dog, which was now chewing his tail. The old woman waved goodbye and shut the door, and Mr Thundermug, succumbing once more to the terrible pain, sprawled on the floor of the taxi.

During the journey, however, he recovered a little, and by the time the taxi arrived at the surgery, and the driver had extracted the banknote that the old woman had tucked behind the baboon's ear by way of payment, Mr Thundermug was almost himself. He stalked up to the reception desk, where he fiddled irritably with the bell until the receptionist looked up from her appointments book and told him to stop.

'Who brought you, anyway?' she asked.

'Name of Thundermug,' answered the baboon.

The receptionist stared at him for a moment, and then said, 'Did your owner make an appointment for you?'

The baboon snorted with exasperation.

'Well,' the receptionist said hastily, 'there's no one waiting, so I suppose you could see the vet now if you like. I'll just let him know you're coming. Why don't you go through?' She pointed down the corridor in the direction of the consulting room.

The vet looked carefully at Mr Thundermug as he walked in. 'What seems to be the trouble?' he asked.

'I have a terrible pain in my abdomen,' said Mr Thundermug.

The vet motioned him to lie down on the cold marble counter that stood in the middle of the surgery, and began to examine him: he measured his cranium with a pair of callipers and prodded his belly all over, so that Mr Thundermug winced. 'Is this strictly necessary?' he asked.

The vet smiled disarmingly. 'These are standard procedures,' he explained, 'which facilitate rapid diagnosis of any condition. I am happy to say that you are simply suffering from a severe case of overeating.'

'Impossible,' retorted Mr Thundermug. 'I'm on a strict diet. How dare you make such an accusation?'

'Nevertheless,' replied the vet, 'I have every confidence in the accuracy of my diagnosis, and also in the remedy which I am about to propose.'

Taking advantage of Mr Thundermug's temporary silence, the vet went over to a desk in the corner of the room and opened a drawer that contained an assortment of hypodermic syringes. He selected the largest of these and began to fill it from a bottle marked 'Monkey Bane'.

Mr Thundermug was shocked. 'What are you doing?' he asked.

But the vet said nothing, and instead started to rummage in another drawer for a suitable needle. He found one and fitted it to the syringe. 'Now, this is a really effective remedy for gastric problems such as yours and, indeed, for any other ailment you might happen to be suffering from,' he said enthusiastically. He raised the syringe in the air and squinted expertly at its contents. 'I can assure you that you won't feel a thing. Bend over, please, if you would.'

But Mr Thundermug had already fled.

'I demand proper medical attention,' he muttered to himself, as he walked down the street. Passing a phone box, and noticing that this time there was a telephone in it, he hurried inside, dialled the emergency number and asked for an ambulance. Then he lay down on the pavement to have a rest; he was still in considerable pain.

Soon he heard the noise of a siren, and then the ambulance itself drew up. The ambulance men manoeuvred Mr Thundermug on to a stretcher and lifted him into the back, then drove off at top speed. On the way to the hospital, the paramedic subjected Mr Thundermug to a swift examination, and concluded that Mr Thundermug's condition was not serious enough to warrant an ambulance. He became quite angry, and his colleagues had some difficulty in restraining him, especially when the baboon told him that he wasn't a proper doctor so his opinion didn't count.

At the hospital, Mr Thundermug was dropped off not at Accident and Emergency but at the Outpatients department. This was done so subtly that he did not have time to take offence.

Once again, he had revived somewhat at the prospect of treatment. 'I've come to see the sawbones,' he barked jocularly, when he arrived in the waiting room.

'Ah, Mr Thundermug, the emergency patient,' said a doctor, who had been checking the list on the desk in front of him. 'Yes, we'd been warned about you. Now, I'm afraid I hadn't expected you to be a monkey.'

Mr Thundermug did not reply, so the doctor continued: 'You see, this is a hospital. We don't treat animals. You'd be better off at the vet's.'

'But I've just come from there,' said Mr Thundermug.

'I suggest you go back, then.'

'Do you know what they tried to do to me there?' shouted Mr Thundermug, jumping on to the desk. 'This is an outrage. I must see a specialist. Are you a specialist?'

'Certainly I am,' replied the doctor. 'My field is paediatrics.'

'I suppose that will have to do,' said the baboon, doubtfully. 'Now then, I have a terrible pain in my abdomen. I think it's either gout or syphilis. Possibly both. Anyway, I need some good strong drugs.'

'Mr Thundermug, I'm afraid you are still missing my point, which is that you are a monkey, and we do not treat monkeys in this hospital.'

All the patients and nurses in the room were staring at the baboon with undisguised prurience. It was the opening he had been waiting for. 'This is rampant discrimination,' he shouted, with gleeful rage. 'I realize that I may be – in the narrowest sense of the word – a baboon, but are you really going to refuse me treatment just because I don't look like you?'

The doctor sighed. 'Well, Mr Thundermug,' he said, 'that is correct, actually. I had been going to point out that we don't have the necessary expertise to treat someone like you. You see, I think you are probably suffering from some complicated monkey sickness that we know nothing about. You'd be much better off with a vet or a zoologist.'

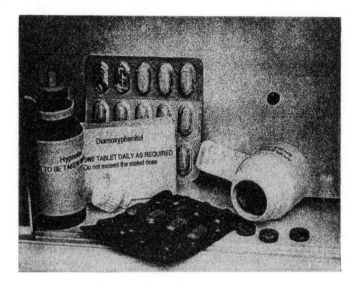

'Look, I just told you—' the baboon started to say, but a fresh attack of stomach cramps seized him: he doubled up in anguish and fell off the desk. By the time he had recovered his composure, the doctor had moved on to another patient.

It was a nurse who helped him to his feet, took his hand and led him, sizzling with indignation, to the hospital pharmacy where she let him make up his own prescription by selecting any medicines he liked. Mr Thundermug chose an assortment of painkillers, sleeping tablets, antacids and laxatives, which the nurse put into a large paper bag for him. Finally she called a hospital porter, and they wheeled him on a trolley, clutching his bag of medicine, to the main entrance, where they put him into a taxi and sent him home.

When he got back to Crofty Creek the baboon emptied all the medicines into a pan with some water, boiled up the mixture on the stove until everything had dissolved and, when it had cooled a little, drank it down. Then he passed out. When he regained consciousness a week later he found that he had made a full recovery.

8

MR FORREST had been trying very hard, ever since his interview with Mr Thundermug, to have the baboons evicted from Crofty Creek. He had been quite confident of his case against them; after all, the baboons were squatting illegally in a condemned house and, what was more, a house belonging to the Council, when they were not even on the housing list. But when he went to consult the Council's solicitor, Mr Gibbons, he found to his horror that the legal expert thought very little of his arguments.

'You can't remove them on the grounds that they weren't on the list,' Mr Gibbons told him, 'because if the house was condemned you wouldn't have been able to put legitimate tenants in there anyhow. And you can't bring a case against them for squatting, because they

didn't force an entry into the house – your monkey was quite right on that point. The makings of a fine legal mind, I should say. Climbing down the chimney – very clever. And you can't get them for occupation of a condemned property either, because by the time you went to see them they'd removed the safety hazard themselves – an infestation of cockroaches, wasn't it?'

'Yes.'

'And they ate them, did you say? Dear, dear, how resourceful. No, whichever way you look at it, it's a very weak case, very weak indeed.'

'What kind of cockeyed reasoning is that?' shouted Mr Forrest. 'These monkeys flout the regulations on at least three counts, and now you say I can't touch them at all? It's disgusting.'

'It's just the way the law works, I'm afraid,' explained Mr Gibbons kindly.

'So what do you advise me to do?'

'Oh, I should let them stay, give them whatever it is they want and try to keep the whole thing hushed up.'

'You'd better do as he suggests,' the head of department said, when Mr Forrest told him the outcome of his meeting with the solicitor. 'Besides, think of the outcry if we threw a pensioner out on the street. Three hundred and seventy-eight years old? That would never do.'

Suppressing his rage and humiliation, Mr Forrest dictated a letter to the baboon, informing him that:

(a) he and his family would be allowed to stay on at Crofty Creek indefinitely;

(b) he was now eligible for an old age pension, to be collected weekly from the post office;

(c) as he was receiving financial assistance from the Council, he would have to comply with its regulations and send his children to the local primary school.

Mr Forrest had insisted on the last point, although the head of department said he did not see what possible use primary education could possibly be to a monkey. 'We must impose some kind of reciprocal obligation,' Mr Forrest told him. 'Otherwise they'll think we're a soft touch.'

As it turned out, the small consolation that this condition should have brought was eclipsed by a final humiliation. Having sent five copies of this letter and received no acknowledgement – unable to read the letters, Mr Thundermug had stored them away carefully, without opening the envelopes, in a drawer of the kitchen table – Mr Forrest was obliged to return to Crofty Creek in person to inform the baboons of the Council's decision.

9

THE BABOON could probably have avoided the educational requirement had he wanted; after all, the authorities hardly expected him to send Angus and Trudy to school. But, actually, Mr Thundermug was getting tired of having the little monkeys around the house all day. They were always getting in his way, clamouring to be fed, or interrupting him when he was trying to have a private moment with Mrs Thundermug, and he thought it would be a capital notion to send them to bother somebody else.

The two little baboons did not seem to be worried at the prospect of education. Hoping to counteract the effect that their appearance might have on their classmates, Mr Thundermug had bought them each a school cap, which he secured under their chins with a string. He went with them to the school gate and returned in the evening to collect them. Waiting by the entrance, he attracted a good deal of attention from the other parents, who discussed him in scandalized whispers.

'Look, a baboon,' one of them said.

On that first evening, the baboon had brought a length of sugar cane to crunch up while he waited, and he offered some to a couple of boys who were pointing at him and scratching themselves. They finished it off between them, spitting out the fibres with relish, but when their father arrived he snatched them away in horror. Angus and Trudy's class was the last to appear, and Mr Thundermug noticed that his offspring had already managed to lose their school caps. He looked carefully into their faces to see whether they appeared any more intelligent than they had been when he left them in the morning. He could not say that they did, but they seemed content enough, and he decided to send them back the next day.

Mr Thundermug arrived punctually every afternoon to collect the children, who walked hand in hand out of the school gate each time with the same impassive expression. Then, at the end of their first week, a young teacher came out with them, holding one end of a cord, the other end of which was attached to Trudy's ankle. Seeing the

baboon, she hurried up to him. 'Are you their father?' she asked.

Mr Thundermug considered making a facetious comment, but decided against it. The teacher had a lovely thick mane of yellow hair. 'I don't deny it,' he said.

'Oh, thank goodness!' she exclaimed. 'I've been looking for you all week. I don't have your telephone number –'

'I'm ex-directory,' the baboon told her soberly.

'– and these two keep giving me the slip. I try to follow them at the end of the day, but they're too quick for me.

They climb out of the window, you know. That's why I tied this cord to Trudy's foot – I hope you don't mind.'

'Is something wrong?' asked Mr Thundermug. 'If they don't behave themselves, just let me know, and I'll give them a good walloping. Or you can do it yourself, if you like.'

'No, no,' the teacher said. 'In class they are very well behaved, almost subdued in fact.' She looked down at the two little baboons, who were squatting patiently on the pavement.

'Well, then,' asked Mr Thundermug, 'are they mentally retarded? I often suspected Angus here might be a few bananas short of a birthday cake, if you know what I mean.' He tapped his forehead significantly.

'It isn't that either,' said the teacher. 'It's partly that I've been very curious to meet you ever since I first saw these two. I've met all the other children's parents, you know.'

'I see,' said the baboon. 'Well, my name's Mr Thundermug, delighted to meet you.'

'Miss Angela Young,' replied the teacher, grasping his delicate fingers. 'I'm in charge of the primary curriculum at this school, and I'm also Angus and Trudy's class teacher. Now, the problem is nothing to do with their behaviour or their intelligence, but – I'm not really sure how to say this, because I've never seen anything like it before – perhaps the unsettling effect they have on other students. You see, I've always thought the children in this class were fairly bright, but all this week they've been acting like wild animals.'

Mr Thundermug snorted.

'Yes,' the teacher continued, 'there's one boy who's terribly intelligent but rather shy, and since Angus and Trudy joined the class he's been walking about on all fours. He was making quite good progress in reading – and in arithmetic – but in the last few days he's been more interested in chasing cockroaches and pulling his classmates' hair.'

'Probably looking for fleas,' Mr Thundermug said. 'So my brats are the ringleaders in some kind of playground Mafia, are they? Well, what do you expect me to do about it? They're your responsibility now, you know.'

'I just wanted to see if I could get to the bottom of the problem,' explained Miss Young. 'Often I find these things can be cleared up when I meet the parents. And, in fact, I do have a suggestion. If you're not too busy during the day, perhaps you might like to come and sit in on Angus and Trudy's lessons. Quite a lot of parents do that in the first few weeks. It helps the children to settle down.'

Mr Thundermug replied that his schedule was full – positively crammed.

'In that case, perhaps your wife – '

'Oh, my wife,' said Mr Thundermug, uncomfortably, 'my wife, er – that is, she doesn't get out much. Yes, perhaps I could find the time, after all. Are you – are you teaching them to read, by any chance?'

'Of course,' said Miss Young. 'It's a core element in the curriculum. Why do you ask?'

'Just making sure,' said Mr Thundermug.

THE NEXT DAY, and every day after that for several weeks, Mr Thundermug accompanied the two little baboons into Miss Young's classroom and squatted on a pouffe in the story corner while they had their lessons. If he thought he saw them 'stepping out of line', as he put it, he would bare his teeth and thump his chest until his ribs rattled. This terrifying display of paternal author-ity had a sobering effect on the entire class, including Miss Young, who eventually begged the baboon to restrain himself. In fact, his antics may not have been prompted by anger at all, but rather by boredom at sitting for hours on end in the classroom with nothing to do. Perhaps he was also frustrated at being surrounded by so many enticing books which he could not read. After a few days he started to creep out of the story corner and sit attentively at the back of the class whenever the lessons were dedicated to reading.

His extraordinary linguistic gifts enabled him to master the alphabet without difficulty; he progressed through the reading course extremely fast, devouring everything from *Stories for Little Girls* to *Practical Zoology*, and by half-term he had returned to his pouffe in the corner, where he sat mulling over the obituaries in the *Evening News* and occasionally casting a stern eye at his offspring over the top of the newspaper. Miss Young was so impressed by the baboon's rapidly acquired erudition that she invited him to dinner in order, she told him, to draw up an independent study plan suitable for an adult male baboon and in keeping with the latest pedagogical theories.

The study plan was duly agreed; but Mr Thundermug's liberal education was soon interrupted. According to their half-term report, Angus and Trudy's behaviour had been 'consistently disgraceful', and they had exercised a demonic and corrupting influence on their impressionable young classmates. It was true: one break time Miss Young invited the baboon to look out of the classroom window at the playground, where several of the children were hopping about and gibbering like apes. 'Several of my best students have regressed to a primeval state, and lost the ability to speak. One boy has gone to live up a tree and refuses to come down,' she told him sternly. A few days later Mr Thundermug received a letter from the school, informing him that Angus and Trudy were going to be expelled, or 'permanently excluded', as the headmaster threateningly put it, with immediate effect.

After a few weeks Miss Young was able to report that most of the children who had been affected by the company of Angus and Trudy were making excellent progress and had recovered their civilized veneer. Only one boy had refused to respond to treatment and remained permanently simian: after raiding a greengrocer's store and making off with the entire stock of Philippine bananas he had been sent to a residential home for the irretrievably insane.

The little baboons never returned to school, and the Parent-Teacher Association maintained its unqualified disapproval of Mr Thundermug, but his dinners with Miss Young had become a regular event. The baboon would wait for her outside the school gate on the evenings when they were to dine together, braving the parents' glares and the children's shrieks of amusement.

10

PERHAPS it seems strange, but none of Miss Young's friends was surprised when they heard that she had fallen in love with a baboon. They were not by nature inquisitive or prying, but her private life had been for many years completely without interest for the prurient. While they committed various indiscretions, came weeping to her on a regular basis and were perhaps less lonely than she was, Miss Young had not mentioned a lover, a fiancé or a husband in all the time they had known her. Her friends never found, in her talk or her behaviour, the germ of an idea around which an exotic past or even a scandalous rumour could be constructed. She let nothing slip; hers was the supreme discretion of a teacher who has convinced her students that she only exists between nine in the morning and four in the afternoon, and that during the holidays she sleeps in a box in the staff room. And so when her friends saw her with Mr Thundermug it did not seem out of character for her to have fallen in love with a baboon; it was enough of a departure for her to have fallen in love with anyone.

In any case, perhaps 'fallen in love' was the wrong way to describe her feelings towards him. She invited him to her house for dinner, made tea, discussed current affairs with him and brought him pots of home-made jam, but perhaps her attentiveness was not much different from any teacher's interest in a favourite pupil. All this Mr Thundermug accepted graciously, and was reasonably well behaved in his turn. His interest in her appeared to be primarily intellectual; they would stay up late into the night pointlessly disputing the most varied topics, from whether fleas can hear to the best method for making puff pastry – exercises which provided both of them with a strange gratification. In fact, the baboon had a kind of rough, old-fashioned courtesy in his manner towards women, which Miss Young at least found very attractive. He was rather like a bluff country squire who used at one time to be quite well-mannered, but has spent too much time among the sugar beet without stimulating or fashionable company, the kind of man who always has straw clinging to his jacket – and, indeed, Miss Young always had to pull grass and other debris out of the baboon's coat when they went anywhere together. He would hold doors open for her and bow to her friends if they met in the street, and insisted on carving the boiled bacon joint at supper, even though she did it rather better than he could, because the knife was too big for his fingers. In the evenings he would sit beside her, staring into the fire and stroking his whiskers thoughtfully. What did it matter that he picked his nose or scratched himself; she knew that he did it out of absentmindedness, and besides, many men had similar habits. Actually, this rough, animal side of his nature rather appealed to her, and certainly it impressed her friends enormously: they would pass remarks, when he seemed not to be listening, about the thickness of the hair on his arms or his wiry prehensile toes, and they tried not to stare with too obvious fascination at his flaming red buttocks when he shifted in his seat, although he did it entirely for their benefit.

Occasionally, if he wanted to show proof of particular affection, Mr Thundermug would sidle up to the teacher as they sat together on the sofa and stroke her hair with his long, delicate fingers, just as he used to groom and pick the lice out of his wife's coat. This had startled Miss Young at first, but he did it so rarely and with such wistful sincerity in his eyes that it always made her tremble with delight, although she was careful to preserve the severe straight face which she had been taught to adopt at her teacher-training college. She was supposed to reciprocate by feeding him grapes or pieces of apple, which she lowered gingerly between his open jaws; or he would stretch out luxuriantly on the sofa while she stroked the warm, tender skin of his chest, which reminded her of chamois leather.

11

EVERY YEAR, in the last days of July, the city was at the mercy of its special microclimate. Incontinent, boiling clouds sucked up water from the surface of the river and carried it a few hundred yards before dumping it on the cracked tiles and crumbling Tarmac of the city below. A huge volume of water would fall in the space of a few minutes; the cycle was so rapid that the rainwater, which the poorer citizens collected in tubs and pails, still seemed to taste of the river. Afterwards the sun came out and the city steamed gently under its vicious rays, while through leaky cisterns, clogged drains and brimming gutters the water found its way back to the river in time for the whole process to be repeated a week later. In this climate fruit rotted before it ripened, wounds festered and drying clothes blossomed with mildew in several hideous

shades. Every year, in fact, new and spectacular kinds of mould would be discovered and rushed to the university laboratories for registration.

Miss Young had gone, as she did every year, to spend the summer holiday with her family in the country, leaving Mr Thundermug alone in the drowning city. He spent much of his time brooding in the kitchen of Crofty Creek, venturing out in the brief intervals between cloudbursts for a cursory inspection of the neighbourhood dustbins. On the morning of a particularly heavy downpour the baboon was squatting in his usual place on the kitchen table and staring out of the window: his wife was asleep upstairs and his children at large somewhere in the flooded streets, having slipped out through the cat-flap. The rain streamed down the glass, little pools of water formed on the window-sill and steam rose over the garden outside. Through the descending volumes of water the rosebushes appeared like undulating seaweed and for a moment Mr Thundermug imagined himself the victim of a shipwreck, somewhere in the depths of the sea: he wondered if it would be possible to grow gills as easily as he had developed his faculty of language. Before him, plastered to the tabletop, was a sodden letter.

The bones of Mr Thundermug's face were long by design and, as I have mentioned, his features were those of a lugubrious Victorian thinker, but today they had a particularly grave aspect, as though he had just uncovered a scandal in the higher ranks of the Liberal Party. The letter had arrived in the post that morning; it came once again from Mr Forrest of the City Council.

The Council had reason to believe that he was keeping a number of monkeys in his house. Was he aware that, without a permit, this was illegal, and also that any mistreatment of animals would be taken very seriously by the Animal Welfare Department? The letter finished with a reminder that monkeys were sensitive and exotic animals, and recommended that if Mr Thundermug really was intent on keeping them, he should arrange for an expert from the local zoo to visit every three months or so to examine such things as their teeth and bowel movements, and to check that he was looking after them properly.

Mr Thundermug's expression was grave because he suspected that this sudden concern for animal welfare on the part of the Council was really evidence of its tireless cunning. With the application of simple logic Mr Forrest must have concluded that since Angus and

Trudy had stopped attending school, it was no longer justifiable to regard them as anything other than animals: animals in need of protection from any possible ill-treatment. The same would be true for his wife as well, Mr Thundermug reflected sadly; after all, she had not learnt a word of human language, and she remained essentially the same fine-boned, silver-maned baboon that she had been on the day when he first met her.

Mr Thundermug's first impulse on receiving the letter had been to eat it and pretend it had never arrived. All his life he had followed the Laws of Nature, and under the Laws of Nature this would have been a perfectly reasonable thing to do. But now, as he knew, he was subject to Human Law as well, which tells us, among other things, never to ignore a letter in a brown envelope or a man like Mr Forrest.

After reading the letter for a second time, therefore, Mr Thundermug went round to the pet shop, where he discovered that the nearest thing they had to a baboon permit was a dog licence.

'Will that do?' he asked doubtfully. 'The letter specifically told me to get a baboon permit.'

'This is a very comprehensive licence,' the manager

told him. 'I'm sure it will cover baboons as well. It just depends on how you fill in the details. Have a look for yourself.'

'"Name of Owner. Name of Dog",' Mr Thundermug read, '"Type of Dog". I see. I'll put "Baboon", shall I?'

'No, no,' the manager said. 'You have to choose from the list they give you – look: "Small Dog", "Dog", or "Large Dog".'

'What should I put, then?'

'I'd put "Large Dog", if I were you. I'll just stamp it for you . . . there you are. Before you go, can I interest you in a sack of Baboon Pellets? They contain all the vitamins and minerals your baboons need to keep them happy and healthy, with strong teeth and a glossy coat. No? All right. But don't blame me if they get scurvy.'

The baboon splashed his way home through the waterlogged streets, musing on the injustices of Human Law. Miss Young had once told him that the law was made for reasonable men and, provided he had no criminal inclinations, there was nothing for him to worry about. But Mr Thundermug was not a reasonable man: he was an unreasonable monkey, and complying with the demands of Human Law was putting him under considerable strain.

When he got back to Crofty Creek he wedged the back door open and lay down on the cool tiles of the kitchen floor. It was still raining. Spray drove in through the open door and settled refreshingly in the hairs of his mane. He rested his chin on the doorstep and inhaled the rank vegetable scent of the garden.

12

MISS YOUNG liked to watch Mr Thundermug when he came to her house in the evenings. She liked to see him pulling her books one by one out of the bookcase with an air of extreme studiousness, leaving them strewn across the rug; or sitting on the table at mealtimes with a napkin tied under his chin (to keep the crumbs out of his mane), while he carved the joint; or stalking up and down along the back of the sofa, his tail held stiffly in the air like a cat's.

It was odd, she reflected; when you thought of it, he was actually walking around naked – and not just in her house, where in any case she would have allowed him a certain degree of liberty. Often she used to watch him through the window as he clambered over her front gate and raced down the path to jangle the doorbell. The thought of him walking the streets in that state and then standing on her doorstep gave Miss Young a curious feeling.

She remembered a studio photograph she had once seen of a family of chimpanzees, posed in front of a painted backdrop of the sun setting over the sea. The mother was dressed in a summer frock with a pair of white court shoes on her feet, while the father had been buttoned into a three-piece pin-striped suit and wore a flashy bow-tie, with a top hat askew on his head. A baby in a bulging nappy sat on the mother's lap. Round its neck it wore a pink bib, which nearly covered its remarkably hairy chest, and it had a dummy in its mouth.

Miss Young had been very struck by this picture, and wondered if it would be possible to dress Mr Thundermug in a similar way. A bow-tie would be ridiculous, of course, but she thought he might look quite dashing in a suit. She also thought people might not stare so much when they went out together if he was wearing clothes. After all, if she went into town with a man who had no clothes on, she could hardly expect people not to stare.

The next time Mr Thundermug came to see her, she suggested he might like to try on some old clothes of her father's. The baboon good-naturedly agreed. 'If you think they'll fit,' he said, and Miss Young went to fetch the suit from her wardrobe, where it had hung ever since her father's death a few years before. It was a fine suit, tailor-made, with a silk lining, but while Miss Young's father had been a small man, there is still a considerable difference in size between a small man and a large baboon such as Mr Thundermug. Besides this, there was the difference of posture and body shape: Miss Young's father did not usually walk about on all fours, nor did he have a tail.

The suit was given up as impractical, but Miss Young was not yet prepared to abandon her idea. She took the suit back upstairs and returned with some of the clothes she had worn as a little girl: a blouse, a knitted cardigan with a design of mushrooms and rabbits, and a gingham skirt. 'Here,' she said, 'these should be a better fit, and the skirt will leave your tail free.'

The baboon, who was rather enjoying this bizarre game, allowed Miss Young to button him into the blouse and the cardigan, and pulled the gingham skirt on over his head, adjusting it round his meagre waist. The outfit certainly fitted him better than the suit had done, although the sleeves of the blouse and the cardigan were rather too short and left his wrists exposed. Mr Thundermug paced up and down on the hearthrug, then went to stare at himself for a long time in the bathroom mirror, while Miss Young watched over his shoulder. 'No,' he said finally, 'it's no good. I look too childish.' Miss Young reluctantly agreed, and helped him take the clothes off again. The outfit might have made him look childish, but the sight of Mr Thundermug's tail and backside, as they poked out from beneath the rucked-up skirt, was undeniably obscene.

Miss Young folded up the clothes and took them back upstairs, then she went into the kitchen to make a pot of tea. Later on, when the baboon was about to leave, she found an old raincoat hanging forgotten on a peg behind the door. She took it down and held it up for Mr Thundermug to examine. 'Why don't you try this?' she said. 'It'll be too long for you like that, but I can alter it.' She dashed into the kitchen, returning with a pair of scissors; she cut the coat away slightly below waist height, and handed it to Mr Thundermug to try on.

The coat fitted reasonably well, and the baboon did not look childish in it either, although it could hardly have been said that it made him look any smarter. Battered by countless downpours, it had faded from khaki to the colour of pale sand, and one elbow was patched.

'Wear it next time you come to see me,' said Miss

Young; she helped him take it off and rolled it into a neat bundle, which Mr Thundermug tucked under his arm as he went out of the door.

But the next time the baboon came to visit, Miss Young was disappointed to see him clambering over the gate in the same state of undress as before.

'I forgot to bring it,' Mr Thundermug said, when she asked him about the coat. Miss Young concluded that he must have dropped it in the gutter on his way home.

Later, though, the baboon explained to her that he never wore clothes because he felt they might impede the natural growth of his hair. He also had a secret fear, which he did not mention: it was that the furious scarlet colour of his backside would begin to fade if he did not expose it constantly to the elements.

Miss Young did not mention the subject of clothes again.

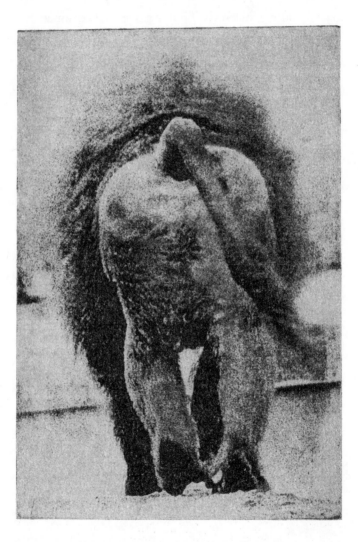

13

It was a clear night in September, and the city was full of people, crowding the parks, the city walls and the mountaintop to look at the full moon. There is no reason why this should not be a solitary activity, but for the people of our city it has always been a social occasion. Families and parties of colleagues gathered with picnics in the dusk to look at the moon and drink sentimental toasts to absent friends. Most of them had been drinking steadily all day and the city, which is usually quiet at this hour of the evening, had the tipsy atmosphere of a festival.

Mr Thundermug and his wife were sitting on the roof of the police station, where there was a tangled arbour of runaway vines and creepers. The full moon gleamed through the latticework. Mrs Thundermug was pulling

leaves off the vine and munching them, while her husband considered the moon, with its pearly lights and sickly shadows. It seemed to him that in the configuration of darker patches on its surface he could see the shape of a monkey. He would have liked to believe it was a baboon, but he knew really that this was just wishful thinking – it looked much more like a gibbon. Now he tried to concoct a fanciful story that would account for the moon's variations in size: the moon was made of some edible substance, and every day the gibbon ate part of it until there was only a sliver left. This edible substance was remarkable, because it was self-regenerating, and after eating almost all of it the gibbon would put what was left in a safe place and fast for two weeks while it grew back to its original size. The explanation had its short-comings: he had never met a gibbon willing to fast for two hours, let alone two weeks, and he was just trying to work out where the gibbon might go while the moon was growing, when he felt Mrs Thundermug pulling at his mane.

Turning to her, he realized guiltily that while he had been thinking, she had eaten all the vine leaves within reach of where she was sitting: etiquette dictated that he should get up and pick some more. He jumped up into the trellis and stripped a couple of branches, scattering the leaves down like confetti over his wife's head. She picked up a few of the leaves and nibbled at them, but not long after he had sat down beside her she was pulling at his mane again. She must want grooming, thought Mr Thundermug, and he shuffled closer to her and began to pick the fleas and lice from her mane. Crunching them up, he fell into a reverie, from which he was woken by the surprise discovery of a caterpillar in the hair behind her left ear. What would a caterpillar be doing in his wife's mane? he wondered, and then he saw that it must have fallen out of the vine above their heads. He ate it without thinking, but it tasted bitter, and no amount of fleas or lice would take away the taste. He nudged Mrs Thundermug. 'Now you do me,' he said, and closed his eyes. But instead of grooming him she began to tug at his mane again.

Mr Thundermug opened his eyes. 'What is it now?' he asked. Was she still hungry? Were there some fleas that he had missed? He could not think what else she might want. He looked into her face for some clue. The little dark eyes under the wrinkled forehead, the elegant muzzle, the surprisingly small white teeth, bared now in a snarl, all stirred the same affection in him as they had

always done, but he could not work out what was troubling her. He thought for an instant of Miss Young, shivered, picked up one of the vine leaves that lay at their feet and chewed it rapidly. Mrs Thundermug turned towards him and began to pick the fleas and lice from his coat. The noise of revelry rose weakly from the city below.

Eventually the baboons curled up together at the foot of the trellis, in the place where the leaves were thickest, while the moon sank between the lattices. Mrs Thundermug fell asleep at once; that was obvious from her breathing and the endearing habit she had of farting in her sleep, but Mr Thundermug stayed awake for a long time, trying to calculate the distance from here to the moon.

14

ONE STEAMING afternoon a few weeks later Mr Thundermug was arrested outside his front door. It was the hottest hour of the day: he was dozing on the front porch, stretched out on the doormat while his wife and children slept upstairs. Two policemen came and took him away. At first they tried to put handcuffs on him, but the cuffs were too big for his wrists. One of the policemen, who was privately exasperated at the idea of turning out on a hot day to apprehend a monkey and subject it to the scrutiny of the law, flung the handcuffs down on the ground at this point and said that they might as well forget it and go home. Luckily the other policeman had a proper respect for orders and a more developed moral character: he picked up the handcuffs, put them on his belt and asked the baboon to come quietly instead.

'Come along now,' he said, 'let's not have any monkey business.'

'I'm afraid that will be rather difficult,' growled Mr Thundermug, scratching himself ostentatiously.

In any case, the baboon did not seem prepared to come quietly. Perhaps he was protesting against Human Law, or perhaps the situation simply appealed to his sense of the dramatic: he screeched and wailed horribly, and bit one policeman in the hand and the other in the leg. Eventually he agreed to go with them when they pointed out that it was nearly tea time, so he could expect refreshments, and promised to let him watch the officers' television.

But the policemen's ordeal was not quite finished: the screeching had brought the rest of the family outside to see what was going on. This enabled the captive to indulge in a tearful farewell to his wife and children, which set the two policemen arguing with each other over the justice of the arrest as they walked the short distance down the street.

When they arrived at the police station the baboon was charged with indecent exposure and cruelty to animals.

'And I hope you understand the gravity of your

situation,' the superintendent told him severely. 'There's no excuse for the indecent exposure that I can see, not for someone with your education, and if there's one thing a jury can't stand it's cruelty to animals. You're looking at a good long stretch.'

The superintendent had recently rediscovered his spare uniform, chewed and reeking and covered with coarse hairs; he could not prove that the baboon was to blame, but he was inclined to be unsympathetic. Mr Thundermug said nothing, however: he was already preparing his speech from the dock.

The duty sergeant took mug shots and paw prints, then sat Mr Thundermug in front of the television with a glass of tea and a piece of sponge cake, while he dealt with the paperwork. After this, the baboon was released on bail; his trial was to begin a week later.

THE POLICE had maintained a deliberate policy of silence concerning Mr Thundermug's arrest and trial, because they did not want bad publicity if anything went wrong and, as the superintendent rightly said, they had better things to do than sit by the telephone fielding stupid questions about monkeys from the general public. Nevertheless, the few details that reporters had managed to gather about the accusations and the defendant were published in the local newspapers, and the case excited a great deal of debate and speculation in our city.

Very few people had really known anything about Mr Thundermug, and as demand for news about him outstripped the supply of truth, it was inevitable that quite ignorant people would set themselves up as authorities. Those who had actually met the baboon were considered better qualified than most to give accounts of him. The two policemen who had made the arrest gave a feature-length interview in a special 'Justice' supplement of the *Police Magazine*, and customers at the post office queued even more patiently than before to have the postmistress harangue them with her opinions of Mr Thundermug's life and character. Naturally there was a resurgence of interest in everything connected with primates: the TV station reran several largely irrelevant documentaries about macaques, marmosets and Neanderthal Man; the *Evening News* obliged with a collectable five-part series entitled 'Monkeys in Profile'; and there was a marked increase in takings at the local zoo.

But all this information did very little to promote intelligent discussion. There was even confusion about what kind of monkey Mr Thundermug was; some people thought he was a chimpanzee, others an orang-utan.

Stranger still was the fact that after his arrest, some of those who had known him professed themselves shocked to learn that he was a monkey. The *Evening News* sent me to interview some of Mr Thundermug's neighbours.

'Imagine,' one of them said, 'he was living in the same street all that time and we had no idea. It makes you afraid to let your children out to play.'

'I know it sounds strange now,' someone else said, 'but he spoke our language so well and he had such nice manners, we didn't suspect anything. I suppose I thought he was a civil servant or something.'

'But he was four feet high,' I pointed out, 'and covered with hair.'

'Well, I assumed he must just be very good at his job.'

15

MR THUNDERMUG'S trial received extensive coverage in the local press. It was as if they were trying to compensate for their failure to provide hard facts at the time of his arrest by giving the fullest possible account of the hearing. And so it is relatively easy to reconstruct the events of the trial, right down to such details as the weather and the design of the blanket (tartan) that Mr Thundermug, standing in the dock, clutched about him as the charges of cruelty to animals and indecent exposure were read out.

'And I've a good mind to charge you with contempt of court as well,' the judge told him. 'It doesn't look like you're wearing anything under that blanket.'

In fact Mr Thundermug had been reluctant to wear even the blanket, but Miss Young had persuaded him that it was necessary. 'You can't walk into a courtroom naked when they're prosecuting you for indecent exposure,' she had said. 'It's just asking for trouble.'

There had been some difficulty over the selection of the jurors, caused deliberately perhaps by the baboon, who insisted on being tried by a jury of his peers. The clerk of the court considered this demand to be a piece of pernicious sophistry, but Mr Thundermug was adamant. 'Twelve silver-maned baboons,' he said. 'I know my rights.' Eventually a compromise was found; the jury was composed of people who were thought to have a special affinity with large primates. The owner of the pet shop was there; the ringmaster of the National Circus; some zoology students; and the coach of the rugby team.

The public gallery was crammed with people – reporters, and those who had simply come for the spectacle. Miss Young was present, but Mr Thundermug's wife and children were not: they had been taken into care shortly after his arrest, in boarding kennels outside the city.

The prosecuting lawyer was Mr Gibbons.

'Who have you appointed to defend you?' asked the clerk of the court.

Mr Thundermug replied that he was going to conduct his own defence.

'What a ghastly pantomime,' said the judge. 'All right, then, let's get on with it. Mr Gibbons for the prosecution, please.'

'This is a straightforward case,' said Mr Gibbons, getting up. 'The defendant is charged with two offences. First, the repeated exposure of his person in a public place, a cause of distress and fright to all who saw it. Second, a much graver charge: the possession of three unlicensed baboons – a protected species, my lord – and the shameful neglect of these animals. I would like to call my first witness for the prosecution, Mr Forrest of the City Council. Mr Forrest' – as the councillor mounted the witness stand – 'I'd like you to clarify a few details for us, please. I understand you wrote a letter to the defendant. Can you tell us what was in it?'

'I wrote to tell him he needed a permit to keep baboons in his house, and also to advise him of the Council's guidelines on how to look after them. Baboons are very sensitive animals, you know.'

'And did he follow your advice?'

'I would say he wilfully ignored it. When I inspected the house after his arrest I found three baboons imprisoned in the bathroom, and the only documentation I could find was a licence for three Large Dogs. Would

91

you describe a baboon as a "Large Dog", my lord? Evidence of a breathtaking contempt for Council regulations.'

'I see. And can you describe how you found these baboons?'

'The bathroom door was shut. I knocked on it and went in, and discovered the animals sleeping in the bath.'

'Had they been cruelly treated, in your opinion?'

'Appallingly so. Anyone with a trace of human feeling would have put them in the bedroom.'

Mr Forrest paused for a moment, then continued: 'As for the indecency, when I went to investigate his irregular tenancy of a Council property, I noticed that he wasn't wearing any clothes. I tried not to let it disturb me, of course, but I understand he makes a practice of it – some people do, you know. I'm only surprised nobody did anything about it sooner.'

'Thank you, Mr Forrest,' said the lawyer. 'No more questions.'

'That all seems pretty clear,' said the judge, sucking his teeth. 'I suppose we'd better hear what the monkey's got to say, though.'

FROM THE MOMENT he arrived in the courtroom, Mr Thundermug had been transfixed by the sight of the judge's silver wig. Surely, he reasoned, anyone with a mane so splendid and – there was no other word for it – baboon-like, must be on his side. The observation had raised his spirits enormously. Adjusting his blanket, he jumped on to the defence counsel's desk, glared defiantly round the courtroom, cleared his throat and began.

'Ladies and gentlemen, members of the jury, Your Royal Highness' – here he bowed to the judge – 'you see before you a poor, dumb animal. A poor, dumb animal, exposed to the harsh glare of human morality by my quite unintentional acquisition of the power of speech. A feat which enables me to stand before you today and plead my case, but which has separated me irrevocably from the society of animals – which has estranged me from my own wife and children. And, having no other choice, I try to adapt to human society – your society, which measures me sometimes by one standard, sometimes by another, but always to my disadvantage. When I behave as a human, I am treated as an animal, and when I follow the counsels of my animal nature I am judged by human standards and found wanting. Hence the charges that have been brought against me.

'But all of you here are more or less animals – some more than others, of course.' Here he leered politely at Mr Gibbons and the judge, who turned brick red with fury. 'And think of the trouble you take to conceal the fact. You wash yourselves not to smell like animals, you wear clothes not to look like animals, and you send your children to school so they can learn not to behave like animals. But which of you, members of the jury, can honestly claim to have succeeded completely in this monumental task? I urge you to look within yourselves before you throw monkey nuts at me.' A dreadful hush had fallen on the courtroom. Encouraged, the baboon continued: 'Have pity on a gibbering ape – that is, on one of Nature's children – and please don't judge me too harshly. Thank you.' He bowed deeply, striking his head on the desk, and scrambled back into his seat.

As he sat down, Mr Thundermug glanced round to see how his speech had been received. He was disappointed that no one – with the exception of Miss Young, up in the public gallery – was applauding, but on the whole he was pleased with the effect: the jurors were conferring in urgent whispers and Mr Gibbons was gasping at his devilish eloquence. Angrily the judge told the jury to go away and consider its verdict.

Nobody who heard Mr Thundermug's speech could have failed to be moved by it, but the case against him was very strong – 'watertight', as the judge put it – and he was found guilty. The court ruled that Mr Thundermug was unfit to look after animals of any kind, and arrangements were made for Angus, Trudy and Mrs Thundermug to be housed permanently in the city zoo. The baboon was also ordered to pay a substantial fine.

This immediately presented a difficulty, because Mr Thundermug did not have enough money. Eventually it was arranged that Miss Young would pay it for him, out of her next month's salary, and that the baboon would go to prison in the meantime.

Mr Thundermug's brief incarceration created un-expected problems for the prison authorities. They were reluctant to put him in a shared cell, for fear of the influence he might exert on other inmates, so they gave him a cell to himself. This caused great resentment among his neighbours, as the prison was severely over-crowded.

On top of this, the warders on Mr Thundermug's wing professed themselves outraged at being given custody of a monkey. The governor was unsympathetic to their complaints, but they vented their frustration on the baboon.

'What do you take us for?' they would demand indignantly, doling out his daily ration of bananas. 'Zookeepers?'

Whether it was due to the warders' attentions or to the solitary confinement, the baboon seemed to react badly to incarceration. He would dash round the cell holding the end of his tail in his mouth and chewing it, or skid about on his hands across the concrete floor like a child on an icy playground. Every now and then he would screech and attempt to overturn his bed. The governor was so concerned that he ordered Mr Thundermug to be put on twenty-four-hour suicide watch – a move which propelled the warders to new heights of fury.

About this time, the baboon received a letter from Miss Young:

DON'T THINK I am surprised not to receive a letter from you. I have been watching some prison dramas on TV recently, and I learnt that prisoners are often denied the use of writing materials. I saw no reason why you should be an exception. I expect the prison routine also makes a lot of demands on your time. Perhaps, though, if you get a chance, you might send me a postcard.

My work at school keeps me busy. I have a new class of children who are lovely, but very high-spirited. Some of them are good students and a credit to their parents, but I don't think I will ever have another pupil as brilliant as you were. I thought of you the other day while the class was having a reading lesson. It made me feel quite sick to imagine you sitting in that cell.

I miss you. As soon as I get my next pay cheque I will make the arrangements with the prison authorities for your release.

I am sending you a box of ginger snaps that my pupils made in their domestic economy class, under my guidance. I hope you enjoy them.

Please take care of yourself. The weather these days is unpleasantly damp, and it would be a bad thing if you were to catch cold in prison. I think you should also try to eat more. In a few weeks we will see each other again. Meanwhile, try not to think of me too much.

I HAVE NO IDEA what Mr Thundermug made of this letter, but the prison warders noticed a change in his behaviour after he received it. He no longer dashed round the cell like a wild thing, or tried to overturn the furniture. Instead he spent a lot of time sitting quietly on his bed, and he remained quite subdued until the day of his release. The prison governor was sufficiently impressed that he called off the suicide watch.

It is not known whether Mr Thundermug received the ginger snaps. Perhaps the warders ate them, and they could hardly be blamed if they had done so. It would have been a small compensation for having to stay up all night.

The prison governor's files contain the last official record of the existence of Mr Thundermug. In the weeks that followed his release from prison, when the fuss had subsided and his story had all but disappeared from the newspapers, I made a last attempt to track the baboon down. I visited, one after the other, the various stations in his progress: Crofty Creek, the residential home, the primary school, Miss Young's house, the prison – but my search was unsuccessful. Crofty Creek, as we know, was boarded up and its garden overgrown. The school and prison authorities were uncooperative, and Miss Young was not to be found at her old address.

From time to time, however, there are reports that someone has seen the baboon in such and such a place – too few for the trail to be picked up again, but enough to convince me that he must still be at large somewhere in our city. What follows is a final glimpse.

16

ENORMOUS yellow leaves blew across the roads and littered the pavements, too many to be swept away. It was autumn, and for the first time in several months, Mr Thundermug was wearing the cutaway raincoat that Miss Young had given him. It fitted him no better now than it had on the day he had first worn it: the sleeves were pinned back above his scrawny wrists, but he had been unable to button it round his belly, and the edges flapped and trailed in the mud. He had no illusions that the garment improved his appearance. Nor would he have claimed that it made him look more like a human – he might have been wearing a raincoat, but he was still barely four feet high, covered with matted hair, and he loped along the pavement on all fours. What he did hope was that wearing the raincoat would make him look less like a monkey. He was on his way to visit his wife and children at the zoo, and he did not want to be mistaken for one of the inmates.

The baboon went down one street after another until he came to a district that was being demolished. Everything that could be salvaged had been stacked on the pavements, so that people had to walk in the road. Dull black tiles, powdery bricks, battered doors and casements encrusted with a hundred layers of paint had been carefully sorted under the plane trees. Soon lorries would come to take everything away, under the terms of the private deals that the demolition gangs had negotiated with the builders' merchants. Strings of washing hung between the small trees, which had once stood in courtyards and whose remaining leaves were coated with dust. No one paid any attention to a monkey in a raincoat.

The zoo was laid out in a park at the foot of the mountain, just outside the city. The monkey house was on the far side of the park, and on his way there Mr Thundermug passed a cave full of lions, a bear pit and a couple of elephants, whose keeper was giving them a bath in their enclosure. The sight of all these animals made him feel uncomfortable, and he started to hurry.

When he reached the monkey house, it took him a

little while to find the baboons, because the zoo had a comprehensive collection of monkeys, all separately housed: chimpanzees, orang-utans and gibbons, macaques, gorillas and marmosets. At last he came to the right cage and, staring through the bars, he saw his wife and children. They were the only baboons in the zoo, and they had the cage to themselves. Angus and Trudy were chasing each other, growling and panting, around the cage, while Mrs Thundermug was trying to overturn a rock the size of herself, jumping up and down on it and emitting piercing shrieks, like a cat or a baby.

Mr Thundermug rattled the bars with a stick to attract their attention, but they took no notice. He looked cautiously in every direction, and seeing nobody nearby he took out of his raincoat pocket the huge hand of bananas he had brought with him. At once the baboons stopped what they were doing and scampered across to where he stood. One by one he broke off the bananas and passed them furtively through the bars. The three baboons devoured the fruit with grunts of appreciation. Mr Thundermug watched them intently.

'I may not be able to come and see you again for a while,' he said, when the bananas were finished. The baboons squatted expectantly on the floor in front of him. Before they lost interest he reached his arms between the bars and patted the children's heads. Then he turned away.

It must have been nearly closing time, because from all corners of the park people were streaming towards the exit. Mr Thundermug turned up the collar of his feeble disguise and hurried to join them: Miss Young had invited him to a dinner party at her house that evening, and he did not want to be late. The sun sent long shadows across the steely grass. As he got on the bus that would take him back to the city he could still hear the cries of wild beasts, mingled with the noise of the traffic.

ACKNOWLEDGMENTS

Thank you to Charles Collier, Mitzi Angel,
Richard Bravery, Silvia Crompton, Flora Dennis,
Alexander Masters, Stuart Williams, Paignton
Zoo and the London Print Studio.